THE SCREECH OWL MYSTERIES

The Candy Bandit

Dedicated to
Grant Stuart Williams
and all the other Screech Owls in the world.

Produced by Salem Press, Inc.

∞ The paper used in this book conforms to the American National Standard for Permanence of Paper for Printed Library Materials, Z39.48-1984.

Library of Congress Cataloging-in-Publication Data
Garrett, Sandra G., 1950-
    The candy bandit / by Sandra G. Garrett, Philip C. Williams.
        p.   cm. — (Screech Owl mysteries)
    Summary: The Screech Owls, a group of multi-ethnic children, solve the mysteries of who took the Halloween candy and what happened to Norbert the hamster.
    ISBN 0-86625-502-8
    [1. Schools—Fiction.   2. Mystery and detective stories.] I. Williams, Philip C., 1952-   . II. Title. III. Series: Garrett, Sandra G., 1950-   Screech Owl mysteries.
PZ7.G18465Can   1994
[Fic]—dc20
                                                                93-31882
                                                                CIP
                                                                AC

First Printing

PRINTED IN THE UNITED STATES OF AMERICA

THE SCREECH OWL MYSTERIES

THE CANDY BANDIT

Written by

Sandra G. Garrett *and* Philip C. Williams

Illustrated by

Kimberly L. Dawson Kurnizki

Rourke Publications, Inc.

"R-i-n-n-n-g-g-g!" went the recess bell.

Mei-Li wiggled in her seat. Children from the other classes shouted and laughed as they raced outside to the playground. Mei-Li looked around at her classmates. Everyone in Mr. Adams' room sat glumly at their desks.

"No recess for this class until I find out who opened the Halloween candy," said Mr. Adams. He pointed to the open sack in his desk drawer and frowned. "I also want to know who took Norbert the hamster."

The class had been studying Norbert as a science project. Now he was missing. Mr. Adams sat at his desk and waited. The classroom was quiet. No one said a word.

"Very well," Mr. Adams said. "You will all write an essay on this subject." He wrote on the blackboard, "Why It Is Not Good To Take Things That Do Not Belong To You."

"Now, class," he said, "I am going to the principal's office to tell her what has happened. I hope that the person who took the candy and Norbert will decide to tell the truth when I return."

Mei-Li glanced around at her friends Luis, Jennie, Tommy, Rebecca, and Derek. They looked as miserable as she felt. So did the other kids in the class. They gazed out the window at the school yard full of children running and playing in the cool autumn weather.

Edward spoke up. "I think Luis took the candy. He always carries candy and bubble gum in his pockets."

"I didn't take it," Luis said. "That would be stealing." He looked hurt.

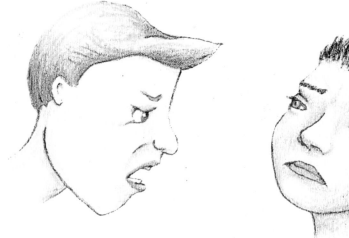

"I think Rebecca took it," Sally said. "She's always eating. That's why she's so fat."

Rebecca blushed. It was true she liked sweets. "I would never go into Mr. Adams' desk," she said. Her eyes filled with tears.

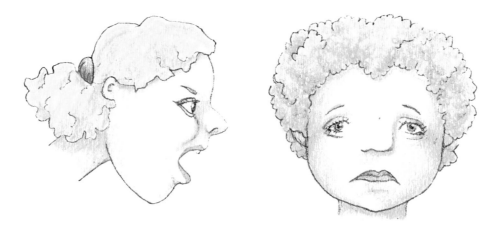

"Jennie loves animals," Edward said. "She probably let Norbert out and took some candy to feed him."

Jennie, who was deaf and mute, read Edward's lips as he accused her of being the thief. She jumped up and stood over Edward's desk, shaking her head. She signed at him.

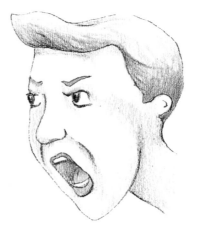

"What's she saying?" Edward mumbled.

"She says she'd never do such a thing without asking," Mei-Li said.

"Besides," added Tommy, "Jennie has lots of pets at home. She knows that candy is not good food for hamsters."

The children settled down to work on their essays. Mei-Li signed to Derek: "Let's call a meeting of the Screech Owls after school. We can talk about who stole the candy and Norbert." The Screech Owls was their club name. Mei-Li, Derek, Rebecca, Tommy, Jennie, and Luis formed the club to solve mysteries.

Derek nodded and signed the news to Luis, Tommy, Rebecca, and Jennie. Sign language was the secret club language. They had all learned to sign from Jennie and Rebecca.

* * * * * *

After school, the children met at their clubhouse. It was an old tool shed in Derek's backyard.

"I've got a plan," Luis said proudly. He showed the other children an old shoe box that he had rigged with springs, wire, rubber bands, and a spray perfume bottle. "I took the perfume out and filled it with vinegar and fish oil. It really stinks. Anyone who tries to get in the shoe box will set off

the sprayer and will get hit by the smelly oil."

He stuck his hand in the shoe box and the oil suddenly sprayed the front of his Baltimore Orioles tee shirt. It was one of his favorite shirts, because he wanted to become a catcher for the Orioles baseball team when he grew up. The others laughed until they smelled the fish oil. Then they groaned.

Rebecca opened the door of the clubhouse. "Whew, that smells awful," she said. "I'll need to bring over some of my homemade rose potpourri to get rid of the stink." Rebecca knew all about plants and flowers and liked to grow them and make potpourri with them.

"How are you going to get the thief to put a hand in that box?" Tommy asked.

"We can rig it up inside Mr. Adams' desk drawer," explained Luis.

"I don't think we should open Mr. Adams' drawer," Mei-Li said. "What if he sees us? He'll think we're the thieves."

"We could go now," said Rebecca. "Mr. Adams is

probably gone, but the school's still open while Mr. Bowman cleans it." Mr. Bowman was the school janitor.

"We'll post lookouts," said Luis. "Derek can help me."

"Let's vote on it," said Rebecca. "Who's in favor?"

Everyone's hand went up except Mei-Li's.

"Come on," said Derek. "There's no time to lose."

* * * * * *

The children rode their bikes to the school yard.

"Look," said Luis, pointing toward the parking lot. "Mr. Adams' car is gone."

"I still think that this is a bad idea," Mei-Li said.

"You'll see," said Luis.

Mei-Li and Tommy stayed outside to watch for Mr. Adams. Jennie stood in the hallway, where she could see Mei-Li and Tommy.

Derek and Luis sneaked back into the classroom. They began setting up the trap in Mr. Adams' desk drawer. Rebecca stood near the classroom door. She was ready to send Jennie's signal to Derek and Luis if Mr. Adams came back.

"That should catch the candy bandit," Luis said when they had finished working on the drawer.

"Uh oh," said Rebecca. Jennie was waving her arms back and forth.

"Mr. Adams is back!" Rebecca cried.

Derek, Luis, and Rebecca ran to the closet and hid inside. They left a small crack in the door so they could look out.

Mr. Adams walked into the room and sat at his desk. He was grading papers.

"Oh no," whispered Derek. "This could take forever."

"What if he opens the drawer?" Luis asked nervously.

"Keep your fingers crossed," Rebecca said.

They waited impatiently for Mr. Adams to finish.

"My legs are tired," Luis complained softly.

"Sit down," Rebecca said.

"I tried, but there's no room with all this junk."

Derek looked at the clock on the wall behind Mr. Adams' desk. It was five o'clock.

"It won't be much longer now," he said. "He'll have to eat dinner soon."

"Derek, did you touch my foot?" Rebecca asked.

"No, why?"

"Something scratched my sock," she said.

"Your foot's probably going to sleep," Derek said. "We've been standing here a long time."

"My feet feel numb, too," said Luis.

"I don't know," Rebecca said. "It sure felt like something tickled my ankle."

Just then, Mr. Adams looked at his watch and got up. He piled the papers in a neat stack on his desk, put on his coat, and left.

Derek looked at his watch. "Ten minutes after five. My dad is going to wonder where I am. He's taking me to his office at the college tonight to try the new computer." Derek was very interested in computers. He also liked to collect insects for his bug zoo.

"I'm starving," said Luis. "I thought he'd never leave."

"Let's go home," said Rebecca.

As they walked outside to the sidewalk in front of the school, Tommy, Jennie, and Mei-Li ran up.

"What happened?" Tommy asked.

Derek told them about their adventure in the closet as they pedaled their bikes home.

* * * * * *

The next morning, the Screech Owls arrived at school early. They walked around the room sniffing, but they did not smell fish oil on any of their classmates.

"I guess no one sprang the trap," Luis said to Derek as they sat down.

Mr. Adams sat down at his desk. "All right, children, take your seats. I'm going to check my desk drawer to see if our burglar visited us again." He reached for the knob on his desk drawer.

Luis jumped up.

"Wait, Mr. Adams," he shouted, but he was too late. Once the drawer was opened, the perfume bottle sprayed a stream of smelly oil and vinegar all over Mr. Adams' neat white shirt.

"What in the world!" Mr. Adams wiped at his shirt.

All the children laughed except the Screech Owls. They looked at each other and wondered what to do.

"Who put this thing in my drawer?" Mr. Adams said with a glare.

The class was silent.

"I'm waiting," Mr. Adams said.

Luis and Derek stood up. "We did it, Mr. Adams," Derek said.

"All we wanted to do was catch the candy bandit," Luis said.

"We didn't mean for it to get you," said Derek.

"You can explain that to the principal," Mr. Adams said. He brushed the front of his shirt with a tissue. The whole room smelled like fish oil.

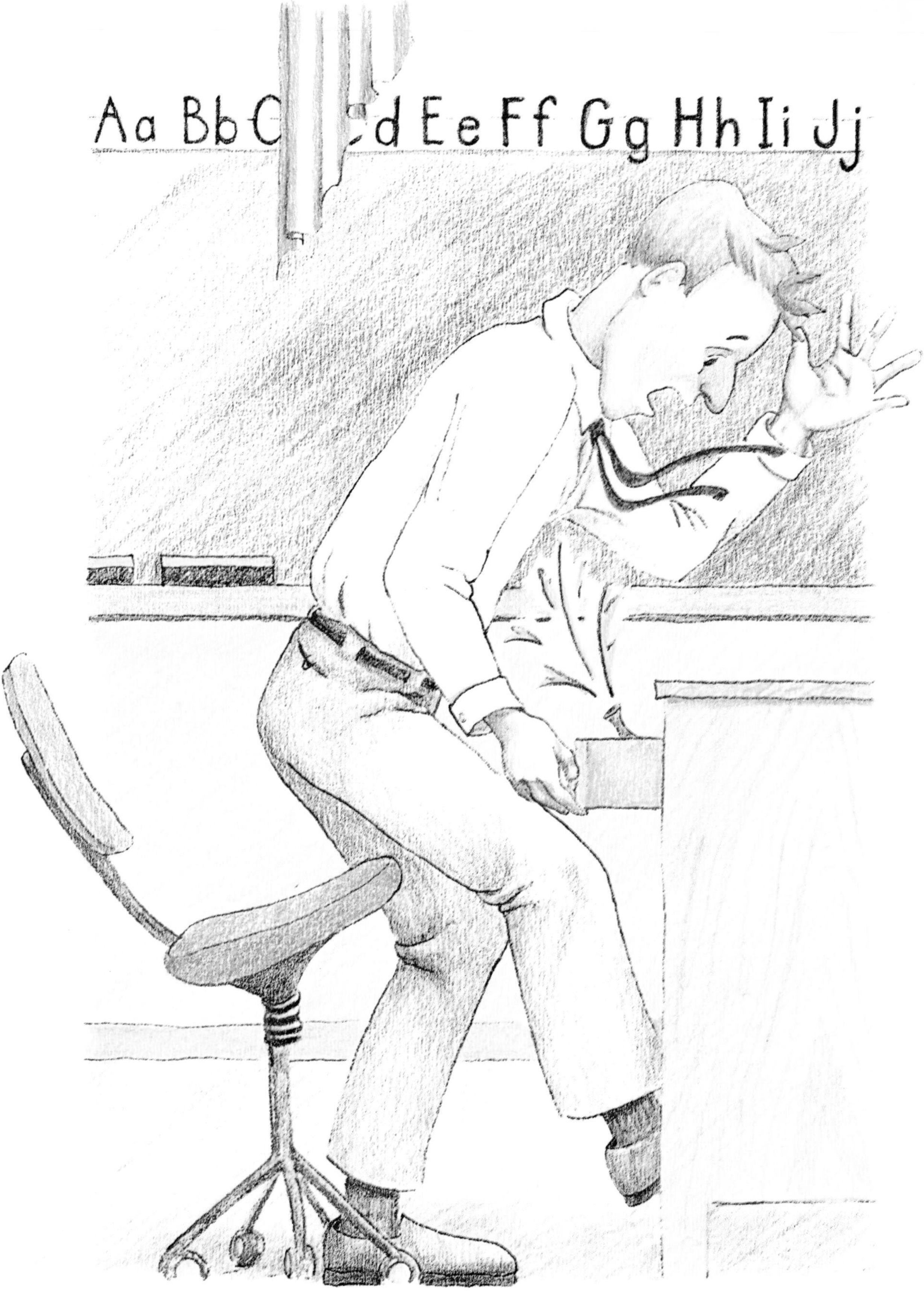
Aa Bb C dEe Ff Gg Hh Ii Jj

Derek and Luis slowly walked down the hall to the principal's office. "Do you think Mrs. Kline will tell our parents?" Luis asked.

"I don't know," Derek replied. "All we can do is tell her the truth and the whole story."

Derek and Luis had never been to the principal's office before. They told the secretary that Mr. Adams had sent them. The secretary led them into the principal's office and told them to sit in two chairs facing Mrs. Kline's desk.

Mrs. Kline looked up from some papers she was reading. She took off her glasses and stared at the boys.

"Well, boys," she began. "What brings you here?"

She listened gravely as Derek and Luis explained about their trap to catch the candy bandit. When they got to the part about Mr. Adams getting sprayed with vinegar and oil, the boys noticed that Mrs. Kline's lips were twitching. She looked like she wanted to smile.

"I can see you were trying to be helpful," she said. "You didn't realize your trap would backfire like that. Still, you really should not sneak into the school building after school is out."

"We just wanted to catch the bandit," Luis said. "It's no fun missing recess and writing essays."

Mrs. Kline shook her head. "What if Mr. Bowman, the janitor, had accidentally locked you in the building all night? Your parents would have been very worried about you."

The boys apologized and promised not to do it again. Mrs. Kline sent them back to class.

"We'd better call another meeting of the Screech Owls," Derek said as they walked back to their classroom.

* * * * * *

After school, the club members met at their clubhouse and discussed other ideas. "We could leave some powder on the floor under Mr. Adams' desk drawer, and I could track the bandit's footprints," Tommy said. Tommy was a Makah Indian and had learned to track from his father.

"What would you do when the powder ran out?" Jennie signed.

"Oh yeah," Tommy said. "Guess that won't work."

"It would have to be something that would stay on the bottom of their shoes a long time," said Luis. "I wonder if red paint would work."

"I don't think Mr. Adams would appreciate having red paint all over the floor," Rebecca said.

Finally, Mei-Li spoke up. "I think we should set another trap."

"Another trap!" Luis said. "You were the one who didn't want to set one before!"

"Oh no," Rebecca said, "I don't want to get sent to the principal's office like Derek and Luis."

"Me neither," signed Jennie, reading Rebecca's lips. "My parents wouldn't like it one bit."

"This trap would be different," Mei-Li said. "We can set up a video camera and aim it at the drawer."

"Who's going to operate it?" asked Tommy.

"No one," said Mei-Li.

"What do you mean?" asked Tommy. "Someone has to turn it on and off."

"We could run a wire from the drawer to the ON and OFF switch on the camera. When the drawer opens, the camera will turn on."

"I get it," Luis said. "Just like the perfume bottle, only with a camera this time."

"That's a very good idea," said Derek.

"Where will we get a video camera?" Tommy asked.

"My parents have one," said Mei-Li. "They let me borrow it sometimes." Mei-Li loved to take pictures. She carried a camera with her wherever she went.

Jennie signed to Mei-Li.

"Don't worry, Jennie," Mei-Li signed back. "We'll get permission this time."

* * * * * *

The next day, Mei-Li went to Mr. Adams and explained her plan. Mr. Adams gave her permission to set up the video camera after school.

Luis and Derek helped Mei-Li set up the camera. "Here," Luis said, "use this." He handed a reel of clear fishing line to Mei-Li.

"Wow," Derek said. "It's almost invisible."

Mei-Li ran the line from the camera to the knob of Mr. Adams' desk drawer and tied it tight. "There," Mei-Li said. "When the candy bandit opens the drawer, he'll switch on the camera without knowing it."

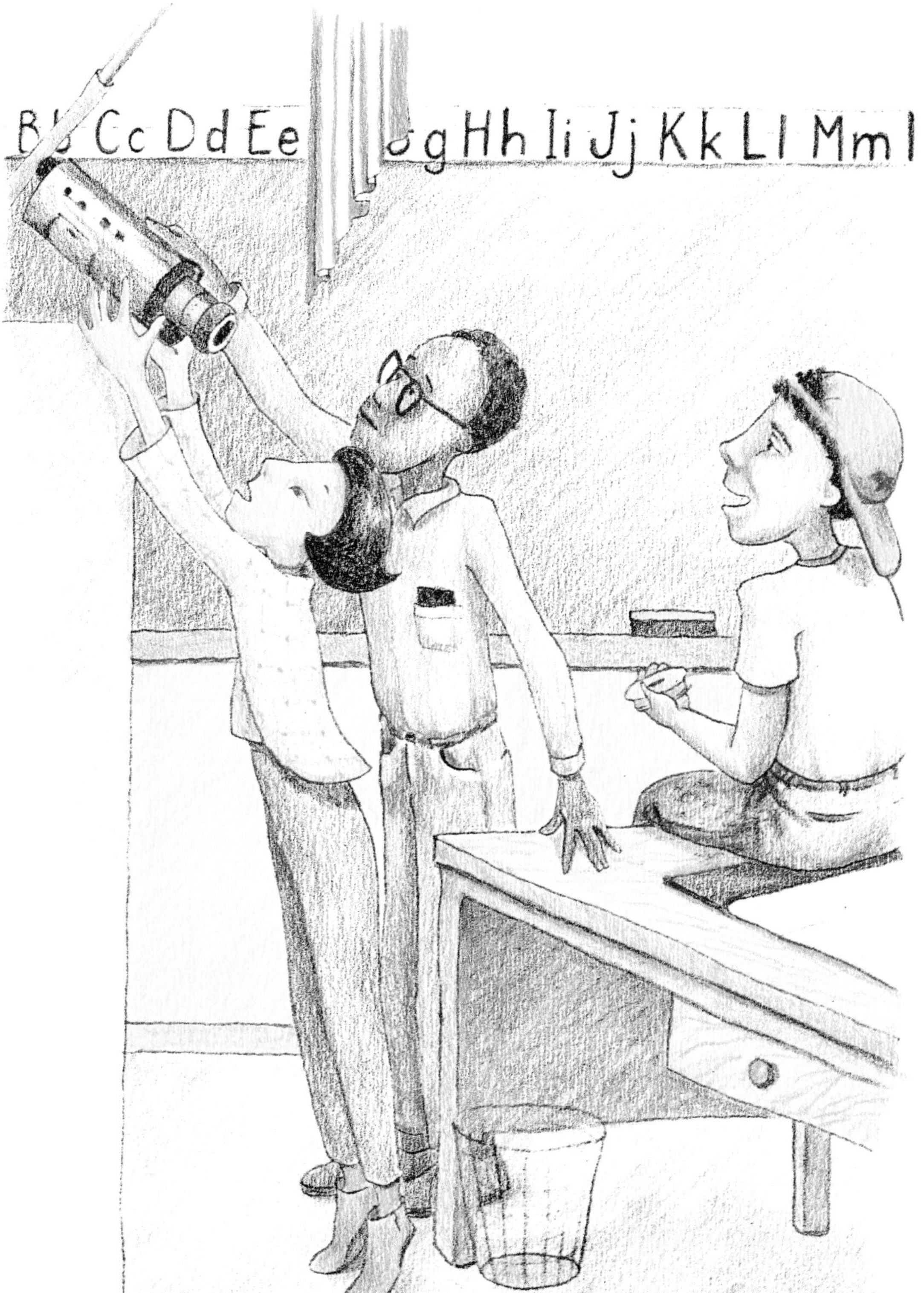
Cc Dd Ee
Hh Ii Jj Kk Ll Mm

"That way we'll get a picture of him," Luis added.

"Let's remember to leave the lights on tonight," Mei-Li said.

"This is much better than having to go around and sniff everybody for fish oil," Derek said.

"I agree," Mr. Adams said. "I don't know if I'll ever get that smelly oil out of my shirt."

Luis blushed. "I'm sorry about that Mr. Adams. Could I take it to the cleaners for you? My mom said to offer."

Mr. Adams smiled. "That's very nice of you, Luis. I'll give it a few more soaks in some soapy water. If that doesn't work, then I'll let you take it to the cleaners." He locked the door behind them and the children went home.

* * * * * *

The next morning the Screech Owls pedaled their bikes as fast as they could to school. Tommy led the charge, blasting a sour note on his old bugle. They couldn't wait to see if the video camera had recorded the candy bandit.

Once everyone was in their seats, Mr. Adams sent Jennie to get Mrs. Kline. A few minutes later, Jennie and Mrs. Kline returned, wheeling a television and VCR on a cart. They set it up in the front of the room, where everyone could see the screen.

"Mei-Li, why don't you tell everyone about the video camera," Mr. Adams said.

Mei-Li showed the camera to the class and explained about the line leading to the desk drawer. She removed the videotape from the camera and brought it over to Mrs. Kline.

"Hopefully this tape will show us our candy bandit," she said.

The principal turned on the television and put the tape in the VCR. She rewound the tape, and then she pressed the button that said PLAY.

Mr. Adams' desk appeared on the screen. The children strained forward to see. The desk drawer was opening, but there was no one there.

"It's a ghost," said one of the children.

A set of tiny paws appeared near one side of the drawer, then a small furry arm. Norbert the hamster craned his

neck around the edge of the drawer and poked his nose
inside. He hooked his front paw into the drawer, opened it
wider, and hopped inside. The children laughed. A few
minutes later, Norbert popped back out. His cheeks were
bulging with candy. He hopped down from the drawer and
disappeared.

"It was Norbert!" the children shouted.

"How did he get out of his cage?" Mr. Adams asked.

"The same way he opened your drawer," Mei-Li said. "He's learned how to turn knobs and open things."

"We should put a lock on his cage once we catch him," said Tommy.

"I wonder where he has been hiding," Derek said.

"I think I know," Rebecca said with a grin. She walked over to the closet and opened the door. "Something scratched my sock when we were hiding in here the other day. It felt warm and furry. I'll bet Norbert has been living in this closet."

Rebecca dug around in the closet for a few minutes. She pulled out a box with pieces of a jigsaw puzzle in it. There was an old knit cap in the box. Rebecca held it out and a little head peeked sleepily over the brim of the hat.

"Here he is. He made himself a nest."

"Look at all the candy wrappers!" cried Luis.

The class cheered as Rebecca took Norbert over to his cage and put him in. Luis dug into his pocket. "I'll wrap some wire around this door until we get a lock," he said.

"Mei-Li, I want to thank you for showing us who our candy bandit was," said Mr. Adams. "Also Rebecca, thank you for finding Norbert."

Mei-Li and Rebecca felt proud.

"I also want to apologize to the whole class," said Mr. Adams. "I've learned an important lesson: Never accuse other people of doing something wrong until you know all the facts."

He smiled and looked at his watch. "I think you all have earned an extra long recess today. Go out and play."

The class clapped and cheered and ran out to the playground. As the Screech Owls ran out together, they smiled at each other.

"Looks like the Screech Owls have solved another mystery," Jennie signed. Tommy blasted the air with his bugle.

Glossary

bandit (*ban* dit): A thief or robber.

gravely (*grayv* lee): Solemnly or somberly, in a serious manner.

impatiently (im *pay* shent lee): In a restless manner; to act without patience or calm.

invisible (in *viz* e bel): Unable to be seen; out of sight.

Makah Indians (mah *kah*): An American Indian tribe that lived along the Pacific Northwest coast, near Cape Flattery in Washington State. The name Makah means "people of the cape." Today, many Makah still live on a reservation along Neah Bay, Washington, while others have moved off the reservation to live in towns and cities.

miserable (*miz* er e bel): Very unhappy.

mumble (*mum* bel): To speak unclearly and in a low voice.

mute (mewt): Not able to speak.

potpourri (*poh* por ree): A pleasant-smelling mixture of dried flowers, leaves, and spices. Potpourri is placed in closets, drawers, and other places to make a pleasing scent.

sign language: Words formed with motions of the hands instead of sounds from the mouth. One language of hand signs is known as American Sign Language.

vinegar (*vin* e ger): A sour liquid that has a strong smell. It is used in salad dressings and in cooking.

We should not make accusations until we know all the facts—to prejudge can be hurtful and does not serve the truth.